Poems about
Weather

Selected by
Amanda Earl & Danielle Sensier

Illustrated by
Frances Lloyd

HODDER
Wayland

an imprint of Hodder Children's Books

Titles in the series
Poems about Families • Poems about Feelings
Poems about Journeys • Poems about Weather

Use this book for teaching literacy

This book can help you in the literacy hour in the following ways:

Children can use the book's contents page, page numbers, poem titles and index to locate a particular piece of information.

They can use the structure of some of the poems as a framework for starting to write their own.

They can examine different kinds of poem from varying parts of the world (see author list below).

They can imagine and write stories, or even newspaper reports, diary entries, etc, based on the poems they've read.

Series Editor: Catherine Baxter
Designer: Lorraine Hayes

First published in Great Britain in 1994 by
Wayland (Publishers) Ltd
Reprinted in 2000 by Hodder Wayland,
an imprint of Hodder Children's Books

© Hodder Wayland 1994

British Library Cataloguing in Publication Data
Earl, Amanda
Poems About Weather. – (Poems About. . .
Series)
I.Earl, Amanda II.Sensier, Danielle
III. Series
808.81

ISBN 0 7502 1930 0

Typeset by Dorchester Typesetting,
Dorset, England
Printed and bound in Italy by
G. Canale C.S.p.A.

Poets' nationalities:

Opal Palmer Adisa	Jamaican
Christina Rossetti	English/Italian
Ogden Nash	American
A.A. Milne	English
Carl Sandburg	American
Richard Edwards	English
Aileen Fisher	American
Kobayashi Issa	Japanese
Matsuo Basho	Japanese
Chiyo-Ni	Japanese
Roger McGough	English

Contents

I wonder

I wonder
who lives
in the sky
way up high
above the clouds

I wonder
what they have
for lunch
and what their
house looks like

I truly wonder
who lives in the sky
way above the clouds
into the endless blue
space
beyond which I cannot see

I know someone
lives up there
because sometimes
just like me
she gets very sad
and tears fall
from her eyes
on top of my roof
on my grass
on my plants
on my head
if I go outside

I wonder
what makes her sad
and why she cries
this rain that
comes from the sky.

Opal Palmer Adisa

4

The wind blew me away

The wind blew me away – it said to me
'Go higher, Jeffrey, go higher, go higher,'
   and I went higher.

Then the wind said, 'Fly Jeffrey,'
and I flew away.
Then the wind blew me down
                        down
                            down,
And it is still blowing me around,
So I must go with the wind.

Jeffrey (aged 4)

Who Has Seen The Wind?

Who has seen the wind?
Neither I nor you?
But when the leaves hang trembling
The wind is passing through.

Who has seen the wind?
Neither you nor I:
But when the trees bow down their heads
The wind is passing by.

Christina Rossetti

Jack Frost

Someone painted pictures on my
Window pane last night –
Willow trees with trailing boughs
And flowers – frosty white
And lovely crystal butterflies;
But when the morning sun
Touched them with its golden beams,
They vanished one by one!

Helen Bayley Davis

Sunflakes

If sunlight fell like snowflakes,
gleaming yellow and so bright,
we could build a sunman,
we could have a sunball fight,
we could watch the sunflakes
drifting in the sky.
We could go sleighing
in the middle of July
through sundrifts and sunbanks,
we could ride a sunmobile,
and we could touch sunflakes –
I wonder how they'd feel.

Frank Asch

Winter Morning

Winter is the king of showmen,
Turning three stumps into snowmen
And houses into birthday cakes
And spreading sugar over lakes.
Smooth and clean and frosty white,
The world looks good enough to bite.
That's the season to be young,
Catching snow flakes on your tongue.

Snow is snowy when it's snowing,
I'm sorry it's slushy when it's going.

Ogden Nash

Outdoor Song

The more it
SNOWS – tiddely-pom
The more it
GOES – tiddely-pom
The more it
GOES – tiddely-pom
On
Snowing.

And nobody
KNOWS – tiddely-pom
How cold my
TOES – tiddely-pom
How cold my
TOES – tiddely-pom
Are
Growing.

A. A. Milne

Winter Morning

On cold winter mornings
When my breath makes me think
I'm a kettle,
Dad and me wrap up warm
In scarves and balaclavas,
Then we fill a paper bag
With bread and go and feed the ducks
In our local park.
The lake is usually quite frozen
So the ducks can't swim,
They skim across the ice instead,
Chasing bits of bread
That we throw,
But when they try to peck the crumbs
The pieces slip and slide away.
Poor ducks!
They sometimes chase the bread
For ages and ages,
It makes me hungry just watching them,
So when Dad isn't looking
I pop some bread in my mouth and have a quick chew.
The ducks don't seem to mind,
At least they've never said anything
to me if they do.

Frank Flynn

12

Fog

The fog comes
on little cat feet.
It sits looking

over harbour and city
on silent haunches
and then moves on.

Carl Sandburg

Cloudburst

There was a young cloud
Who wanted to rain.
Its cumulus* mother said:
'What? Not again?
You're a stupid young cloud,
Without any doubt,
Why didn't you say so
Before we came out?
It's supposed to be summer,
You'll just have to wait.'
The little cloud answered:
'I can't. It's too late.
I'm so full I'm bursting,
I can't keep it in!'

And that's why our cricket match
Couldn't begin.

Richard Edwards

*fluffy white cloud

June

The day is warm
and a breeze is blowing,
the sky is blue
and its eye is glowing,
and everything's new
and green and growing . . .

My shoes are off
and my socks are showing . . .

My socks are off . . .

do you know how I'm going?
          BAREFOOT!

Aileen Fisher

Shower

Fierce
spring
rain
full
gushing
drain
grey
drab
steely
sky
puddled
street
umbrellas
held
Wellies
cars
high
for
make
children
feet
spray
want
birds
out
rain
huddle
harassed
becomes
away
mothers
drops
cats
shout
slows
lie
and
asleep
plants
stops
drink
doors
deep
open
wide
people
step
outside

Moira Andrew

18

Falling Leaves

The leaves in autumn
Swing on the boughs
Pushed by the wind,
Backwards and forwards
Far above the ground.

The wind blows hard
And the leaves let go
Their hold,
Flying over the woods
Like a flock of birds
And brown as sparrows
Flying above the house.

The wind lets them fall
Helter skelter
Towards the ground
Or sets them spinning
On a roundabout;
You can watch them
And try and catch them
Coming down.

They crowd together
By walls at corners
Or chase each other
Up the road.

Sometimes when you open
The kitchen door
A leaf blows in
And lies exhausted
On the floor.

Stanley Cook

The Storm

In my bed all safe and warm
I like to listen to the storm.
The thunder rumbles loud and grand –
The rain goes splash and whisper; and
The lightning is so sharp and bright
It sticks its fingers through the night.

Dorothy Aldis

First Song of the Thunder

Thonah! Thonah!
There is a voice above,
The voice of the thunder.
Within the dark cloud,
Again and again it sounds,
Thonah! Thonah!

Thonah! Thonah!
There is a voice below,
The voice of the grasshopper.
Among the plants,
Again and again it sounds,
Thonah! Thonah!

Anonymous

23

I could eat it!
This snow that falls
So softly, so softly.

Kobayashi Issa

The snow thaws –
And suddenly the whole village
Is full of children!

Kobayashi Issa

Clouds

Clouds come from time to time –
and bring to men a chance to rest
from looking at the moon.

Matsuo Basho

Spring rain;
Everything just grows
More beautiful.

Chiyo-Ni

All Sorts

In March, all sorts of weather.
Winds wait for you round every corner,
Sun shines, hailstones the moment after,
Hoarfrost on gardens, drizzly mornings.

In March, all sorts of colours,
Grey skies and water, violets in woodlands,
Greenfinches on far greener branches,
Speckled trout rising, first butterflies.

In March, all sorts of happenings,
Hedgehogs stroll quietly round the houses,
Rooks squabble, lambs charge at nothing,
Tadpoles grow fatter, evenings longer.

Leonard Clark

Red Skies

Red sky at night
Is a shepherd's delight.
Red sky in the morning
Is a shepherd's warning.

Traditional
Weather Forecast

Snuggles

Work done
for the day
the sun
switches on
the moon
pulls
the clouds
over its
head and
snuggles
right down
into the
cosy bottom
of the sky.

Roger McGough

How to use this book

Poetry is a very enjoyable area of literature and children take to it naturally, usually beginning with nursery rhymes. It's what happens next that can make all the difference! This series of thematic poetry anthologies keeps poetry alive and enjoyable for young children.

When using these books there are several ways in which you can help a child to appreciate poetry and to understand the ways in which words can be carefully chosen and sculpted to convey different atmospheres and meanings. Try to encourage the following:

- Joining in when the poem is read out loud.
- Talking about favourite words, phrases or images.
- Discussing the illustration and photographs.
- Miming facial expressions to suit the mood of the poems.
- Acting out events in the poems.
- Copying out the words.
- Learning favourite poems by heart.
- Discussing the difference between a poem and a story.
- Clapping hands to rhythmic poems.
- Talking about metaphors/similes eg what kind of weather would a lion be? What colour would sadness be? What would it taste like? If you could hold it, how would it feel?

It is inevitable that, at some point, children will want to write poems themselves. Writing a poem is, however, only one way of enjoying poetry. With the above activities, children can be encouraged to appreciate and delight in this unique form of communication.

Picture acknowledgements

APM Studios cover; Frank Lane 5 (M Newman), 6 and 7 (Silvestris); Robert Harding 13 (Adam Woolfitt), 19, 26 (Adam Woolfitt); Still Pictures 11 (B & C Alexander); Tony Stone Worldwide 21 (David Hiser), 22 and 23, 28 (Rob Boudreau); Zefa 8 (M Wright), 14, 17.

Text acknowledgements

For permission to reprint copyright material the publishers gratefully acknowledge the following: Opal Palmer Adisa for 'I Wonder'; Frank Asch for 'Sunflakes'; Curtis Brown Ltd for 'Winter Morning' by Ogden Nash from *The New Nutcracker Suite*. Copyright © 1962 Ogden Nash. Reprinted by permission of Curtis Brown Ltd; Dobson Books Limited for 'All Sorts' from *Four Seasons* by Leonard Clark; Doubleday for 'Clouds' by Matsuo Basho from *An Introduction to Haiku* by Harold G. Henderson. Copyright © 1958 by Harold G. Henderson. Used by permission of Doubleday, a division of Bantam Doubleday Dell Publishing Group, Inc; Felicity Bryan Literary Agency for 'Cloudburst' by Richard Edwards from *The Word Party*. Copyright © 1986 Richard Edwards. Reproduced by permission of Felicity Bryan Literary Agency; Aileen Fisher for 'June' from *Going Barefoot*. Copyright © Aileen Fisher, renewed 1960; Frank Flynn for 'Winter Morning', by Frank Flynn; Harcourt Brace & Company for 'Fog' by Carl Sandburg from *Chicago Poems*; Hokuseido Press for two Haikus translated by R.H. Blyth; Sarah Matthews for 'Falling Leaves' by Stanley Cook; John Murray for 'The Snow Thaws' from *The Autumn Wind* by Kobayashi Issa; 'Snuggles' from *Pillow Talk* by Roger McGough. Reprinted by permission of The Peters, Fraser & Dunlop Group Ltd; G.P. Putnam's Sons for 'The Storm' by Dorothy Aldis from *Everything and Anything*. Copyright © 1925-1927, copyright renewed 1953-1955 by Dorothy Aldis. Reprinted by permission of G.P. Putnam's Sons; Reed Book Services for 'Outdoor Song' from *The House at Pooh Corner* by A. A. Milne. Published by Methuen Children's Books; University of Nebraska Press for 'First Song of Thunder' from *When The Sky Clears* by A. Grove Day. While every effort has been made to secure permission, in some cases it has proved impossible to trace the copyright holders. The publishers apologise for this apparent negligence.

Index of first lines